CALIFORNIA STATE COLLEGE, S

WITHDRAWN

go and hush the baby

go and hush the baby

Betsy Byars

Illustrated by Emily A. McCully

THE VIKING PRESS   NEW YORK

Text copyright © 1971 by Betsy Byars
Illustrations copyright © 1971 by Emily A. McCully
All rights reserved
First published in 1971 by The Viking Press, Inc.
625 Madison Avenue, New York, N.Y. 10022
Published simultaneously in Canada by
The Macmillan Company of Canada Limited
Library of Congress catalog card number: 72–136825
Printed in U.S.A.
670–34270- x   VLB 670–34271–8
3   4   5   75   74   73   72

Go and hush the baby, Will.

It won't take long.

Go and hush the baby,

Sing him a little song.

For he's a jolly good baby,

For he's a jolly good baby,

For he's a jolly good baaaa-beeeeeeeeee—

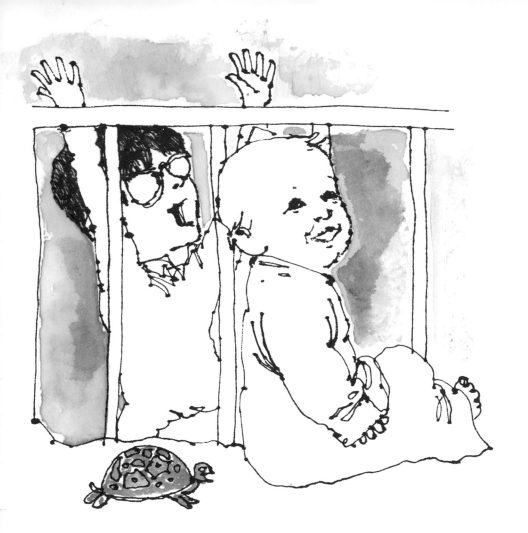

Which nobody can deny!

Bye-bye,

jolly good baby!

Go and hush the baby,

He's crying still.

Play him a game
Or talk to him, Will.

All right, now, we're going to play Cross the Ocean.

You're the little sailboat. See? And I'm the tugboat. This one. Now let's have a race to see who gets across the ocean first. Here we go.

You're moving ahead. You're moving ahead some more. See, here I am stuck on a sand bar and here you are moving ahead. You're moving ahead, moving ahead, moving ahead. You're coming into the harbor!

THE WINNER!

THE CHAMPION OF THE OCEAN!

THE GREAT AND WONDERFUL WINNER!

Wait! Is that the baby?

Go take him a treat.

He's crying again,

Give him this to eat.

I am now going to do for your entertainment a magic trick. In this hand, as you can see, I have nothing. In the other hand, I also have exactly nothing. Nothing in this hand, nothing in that. Now I count. One . . . two . . . three . . .

TA-DAAAAAAAAAA!

Will, I hear the baby. See what's wrong?

Tell him a story, please,

It won't take long.

Once upon a time there was a princess who fell asleep. Nobody could make her wake up. Princes were always coming and kissing her to wake her, but no luck. The princess was fast asleep.

Well, one day a fat jolly prince came to the castle and he went up to the princess, and instead of kissing her he made her laugh by tickling her like that and like that and like that. And she woke up and married the fat jolly prince and there was great rejoicing in the kingdom.

But that's not the end, because one day
the fat jolly prince went on a diet and—

Do you want to hear about the fat jolly
prince and what happened about the diet?

Well, I have to play this game of baseball anyway.

Bye-bye, jolly good baby!